Oink! Moo! How Do You Do?

Oink! Moo! How Do You Do?

A Book of Animal Sounds

by Grace Maccarone
Illustrated by Hans Wilhelm

To B.G.F.
- *G.M.*

Scholastic Children's Books,
Commonwealth House, 1–19 New Oxford Street,
London, WC1A 1NU, UK
a division of Scholastic Ltd
London • New York • Toronto • Sydney • Auckland

First published in the US by Scholastic Inc. 1994
First published in the UK in 1997 by Little Hippo,
an imprint of Scholastic Children's Books.
Text copyright © Scholastic Inc. 1994
Illustrations copyright © Hans Wilhelm, Inc. 1994

ISBN 0 590 54306 7

Printed and bound in Hong Kong

2 4 6 8 10 9 7 5 3 1

Oink! Moo!

How do you do?

Baa! Hee-haw!

It's for us, I'm sure!

Ribbit! Tweet!

There's plenty to eat.

Hoot! Meow!

Let's hurry there now!

Honk! Neigh!

We're on our way!

Cock-a-doodle-doo!

I'm coming, too!

Caw! Cluck-cluck!

We're all in luck!

Gobble-gobble! Ruff!

We've had enough.

Hey! Shoo!

Away with you!

Cheep! Cheep! Cheep!

Quack! Quack!

Ru[

Hee-haw!

Meow!

Oink!

Baa!

Quack-quack!

Caw!

Tweet!

Hoot!

Neigh!

Moo!

Squeak!

Ribbit!

Buzz!

Gobble-gobble!

Honk!

Cock-a-doodle-doo!

Cluck-cluck!

Chirp!

Squeak! Quack-quack!

We enjoyed that snack.

Chirp! Buzz-buzz!

What a good feast it was!

Cheep! Cheep! Cheep!

And now to sleep.

Sheep

Owl

Cow

Dog

Goose

Robin

Donkey

Horse

Bee

Chicke